AN OLD BARN BOOK

First published in 2018 in the UK and Australia and New Zealand
by Old Barn Books Ltd, Warren Barn, West Sussex, RH20 1JW, UK
www.oldbarnbooks.com

This paperback edition published in 2019 by Old Barn Books Ltd

Distributed in the UK by Bounce Sales & Marketing
and in Australia and New Zealand by Walker Books Australia

The illustrations were created in line and watercolour wash

ISBN: 9781910646397

10 9 8 7 6 5 4 3 2 1

Printed in Malaysia

MIX
Paper from
responsible sources
FSC® C012700

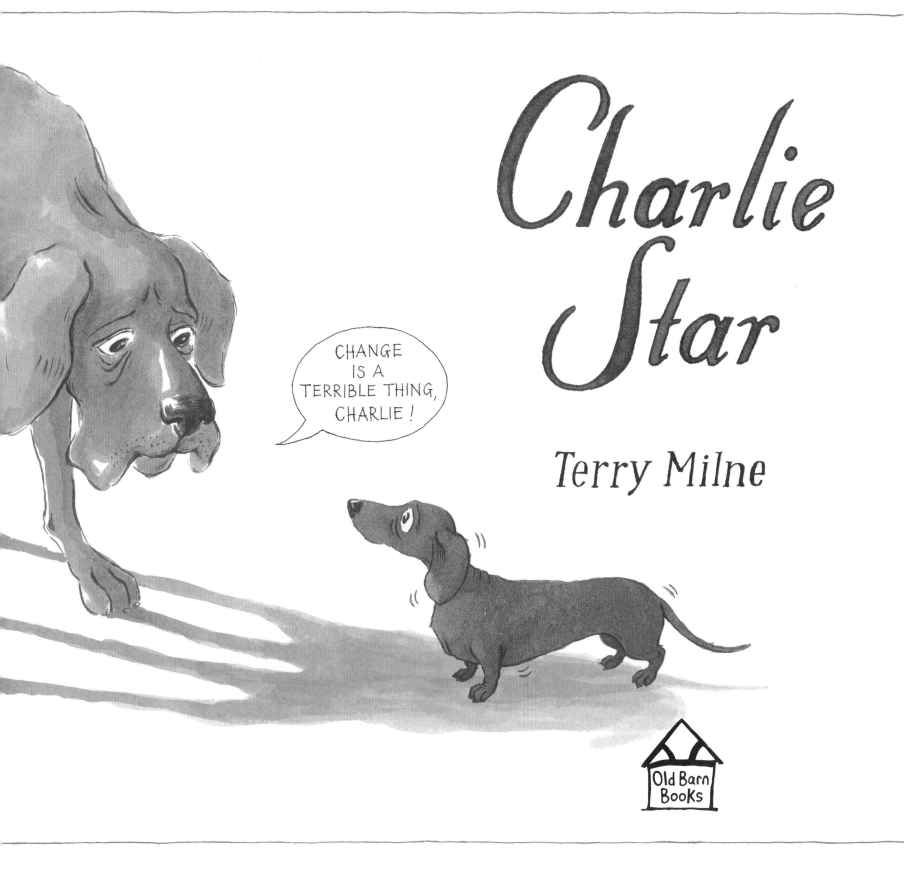

Every morning,
Charlie hopped out of bed.

1...2...3... *Hop* like a flea.

He balanced his toast.

4...5...6... *Charlie* likes his tricks.

And he watered his plants.

7...8...9... *In* a straight line.

Every day, Charlie walked once around the fire hydrant on his way to market,

and always on the same side of the old Oak tree.

Charlie did everything the same, every day.
He was afraid something terrible would happen if he didn't.

At bedtime,
Charlie checked
under the bed...

... and behind
the curtain,
to be certain.

And he arranged his toys in a neat row:

All into bed, Rabbit, Panda, Ted,
to bring good luck, Dog, Doll and Duck.

When at last he lay down,
Charlie thought the same thought
he thought every night:

"REMEMBERED EVERYTHING TODAY
AND THINGS TURNED OUT OKAY!"

Early one morning the phone rang...

TRRRRRiiiNGG
TRRRRiiiiNGG

Charlie leapt straight out of bed
and ran to pick it up.

Said Duck.
Their friend, Hans, was stuck.

"Oh, what bad luck!" Charlie promised to help.

4...5...6... Must do my tricks...

OOPS!

7... 8...9... It's going to be fine.

Oh no... Forgot to water my plants!

Duck led the way. They rushed past the fire hydrant, and went the
<u>wrong</u> way around the old Oak tree !
Charlie wanted to go back to bed and start the day all over again,
but his friend needed him.

"Better late than never!" purred Cat.
"We were playing Hide-and-Seek,"
said Big Bruce.

We tried to ROLL
Hans out of the pipe.

We tried to PUSH him
out of the pipe.

We tried to PULL
him out of the pipe.

Charlie looked anxiously into the dark pipe...

He had an idea.

He picked up one of Duck's feathers and went in.

WOOF WOOF !

TEE HEE

HA HA HA

HO HO

TEE HE

Charlie tickled and
Hans giggled.

He wiggled and
wriggled and jiggled and
giggled until…

"Thanks, Charlie,"
said Hans, "You're a star!"

"Quack, quack, quack!"
agreed Duck.

Then Cat said,
"Shall we play
'Do-this-do-that'?"

"Yeah!"
replied the others.

So they played
all afternoon.

On his way home, Charlie felt so happy
that he didn't mind which way he
passed the old Oak tree.

He flopped onto his bed with a new thought in his head.

"FORGOT EVERYTHING TODAY
BUT THINGS TURNED OUT OKAY."

The next morning,
Charlie hopped out of bed.

1..2...3... *Hop like a flea.*

He balanced his toast.

4...5...6... *Charlie likes his tricks.*

And he watered his plants.

7...8...9... *In a straight line.*

On his way to market, he
went once around the fire hydrant.
Then, for the thrill of it, he skipped any old how past the old Oak tree,
because now Charlie knew what might happen if he went the wrong way...
....nothing terrible, and maybe....

...something

Wonderful !